From The Other Side Of My Mind

From The Other Side Of My Mind

George Mansell

Copyright George Mansell

All rights reserved

The right of George Mansell to be identified
As author of this work has been asserted by him
In accordance with the
Copyright, Design and Patents Act, 1988.
George Mansell
Email: opus65@ymail.com

All rights reserved

No part of this publication may be reproduced, stored in a retrieval
System, or transmitted in any form or by any means, electronic,
Mechanical, photocopying, recording or otherwise, without
The prior permission of the author.

"From The Other Side Of My Mind"
is dedicated to my son and best friend Blaine Mansell
and to the memory of my late son Niall Mansell.
I love you both very much.

Table of contents:

Foreword…page 11
Acknowledgments…page 13
Not Here…page 15
Procrastination…page 16
Time Is…page 17
Book Lover…page 18
Keep It Real…page 19
Assignment…page 20
The Temple…page 21
Hard Times…page 22
Roulette…page 23
Skylark…page 24
Down By The Stream…page 25
Rubato…page 26
Winter Silence…page 27
Star Attraction…page 28
The Great Conjunction…page 29
Sol-Sistere…pages 30 & 31
Snow Moon…page 32
Moon Boy…page 33
Suddenly Spring…page 34
Song Of The Morning…page 35
Full Circle…page 36
Ode To Nick Drake;
(Borrowed Lines)…pages 37, 38 & 39
Not Quite Right; All The Mad Men Revisited
(Tribute To David Bowie)…page 40
Musings On David Sylvian's Orpheus…pages 41 & 42
The Last Farewell…page 43
Welcome To Dystopia…page 44
Deepest Dreaming…page 45
I Love The Sky…page 46
The Space…page 47
Don't Rain On My Parade…page 48
The Enemy Within…page 49
Lowborn…page 50
The End Of The Dream…page 51
I Scorpion…page 52
Wounded…page 53

Table of contents:

The Black Widow…page 54
Child's Play…page 55
Hummingbird…page 56
Elephant On A Tightrope…page 57
Wond'rin' (Memories Of Lee Marvin)…page 58
Limbo…page 59
Broken…page 60
Moonlight Flit…page 61
The Long Walk…page 62
Gone…page 63
New Life…pages 64 & 65
Once I Was A Wildflower Meadow
(The Sad March Of Progress)…pages 66 & 67
Ivo And Laria…pages 68 & 69
Blodeuwedd – Owl Goddess…page 70.
Biography…page 72

Foreword:

George Mansell
is a simply lovely ole chap in his own right,
with his witty sense of humour
and lovable personality.
He has a warm heart and a soft spot for nature.
His way of crafting words into his emotive poetry
leaves the reader wanting more.
In his compilation of 50 poems,
he weaves words in many different subjects,
such as nature, music, and personal struggles.
I really enjoy how he ends many of those pieces,
dealing with life on a positive note.
Please, grab yourself a cup of tea or coffee,
whichever you prefer.
Sit back and enjoy reading
George Mansell's marvelous works
in his first self-publication,
The Other Side of My Mind.
Diona Rodgers

Acknowledgments.

A big thank you to Blaine Mansell
for the cover photograph
and his loving support.
Thank you Alys Kane
for her friendship and encouragement.
Many thanks also to Diona Rodgers
for her wonderful foreword
and friendly support.

Not Here

Nowhere am I
Out of the way
Traces are gone

Hidden from view
Erased from time
Removed from scenes
Every day

Procrastination

Ev'ry day I procrastinate
I don't get much work done of late
I tell myself it's all ok
to put it off for one more day

The work it piles up all the while
but I tell myself, with wry smiles
there's lots of time to get it done
I'll start tomorrow after one

I need routines to do these tasks
no excuses, remove this mask
stop being negative, that's a start
deal with my fears, speak from the heart

Break the jobs down, small is best
take a break, then tackle the rest
and soon it's done, fist pumps the air
I finished a chore, no despair

A moral boost, a special friend
helping me work right to the end
forgive myself when it goes wrong
it's all part of what made me strong

Time Is

Goddesses of life, of time and fate
Hemsut and Shai of African states
in Lakota Etu time personified
Fatia, Ora and Aion, Europe wide
for Germanics, Smaar and Vetr stood
for the fate of all, bad and good
time is immortal, infinite and true
but time is just ticking for me and for you

Book Lover

Open book, a story engrossed
behind a pile of ancient tomes
and I'm in a world of my own
amidst pages of history
caught in a fantastic journey
behind the Greek anthologies
now I'm lost in a maze of words
I can't find my way out of here

Keep It Real

Open your minds to truth
go out into the wilderness
let the nature's light smile on you
it's there to find if you believe

Keep out the fake and false of heart
they're everywhere you turn
but they can not do you harm
if you sit back and let them burn

Assignment

Nothing will ever change
until I've found the alignment
no connection, out of range
what's the purpose of this assignment?

The Temple

You are the temple of my darkness
bringing light where hitherto unseen
I am calm in your blessed presence
letting go the thoughts that disturb me
you are the true focus of my peace
and you are all that quenches my thirst
I am made complete when I hear you
and forever give myself to you
you are my muse, my everything
you are music and music is you

Hard Times

Ragged and weather worn
downbeat and so forlorn
abused and kicked around
doesn't complain
makes no sound
just his bottle and a smoke
loves a smile and a joke
but Joe doesn't mind
he's so gentle and kind
sings old Tom Waits songs
sits there all day long
he'll take food and loose change
no, he's not weird or strange
he once had a career
and a life full of cheer
so be kind and be true
this could one day be you

Roulette

Another game of rum roulette
three days of ruin and regret
stomach pumped in A & E
a state you wouldn't want to see

I can't remember what went on
I said I'd only stay for one
I'm lucky, I'm told, to survive
almost didn't get there alive

I'm not a drinker, it makes me ill
so drink again I never will
please take this lesson from me true
next time you stop by for one...or two

Skylark

It's a hot early evening
late spring in 75
I'm lying flat on my back
on grassland where I lived
I listen to the mesmerising song
of the elusive Skylark
I hear him and a grasshopper too
but I see neither of them

Suddenly I see the grasshopper
as I feel him touch my hand
hot sun heats the ground
on which I've laid so long
I squint to adjust my vision
and then see the skylark clear
hovering as he sings
as grasshopper chirrups away

A thousand feet high in the blue
he parachutes back down below
but for this ten year old boy
it's a sight to forever cherish
suddenly I'm feel less alone
not awkward and uncomfortable
no, I have found pure joy
in the sights and sounds of this day

Down By The Stream

Over the old railway track
and down among the wheat
behind our garden out back
at the end of my street

I lie very still, wait 'til when
I see pond skaters below
with water-boatmen
in the stream long and shallow

Where the water runs bright
crane flies dart all around
dancing their courtship rite
almost skimming the ground

This refuge I would find
that I loved so as a child
both serene warm and kind
and where nature grew wild

Rubato

Swinging

like a red heart beating
pulsating rhythm breaking

drop beat

kick drum

rim shot

cymbal riding

Bassline following
like a chugging train
sax and trumpet
jump in now

Tempo changes
to red hot mood

Singer joins in
scats the tune
slips into her vibe
mojo working overtime

Crowd goes wild
time to dance
swinging rhythm
in town tonight

Winter Silence

Stillness, a frozen winter canvas
save for a lone crow in the distance
again silence
but be still and listen
listen with your entire being
be alone in the moment
in the silence of nature
hear that?
and again?
the beauty of sound
where you thought
there was none

Star Attraction

Clear winter nights
cinematic
celestial
scenes

Orion directly above
my guiding stars

Dark
bitter
cold

I can see myself breathing

Pointing my scope
to the furthest star

In awe
of the wonders around me

Andromeda
in all its glory

Mysterious
enchanting

The Great Conjunction

Jupiter and Saturn cross paths tonight
but I can't see them
the weather isn't right
not seen this close since 1623
separated by just 0.1 of a degree
Jupiter's moons and Saturn's rings
Galileo, Titan and other such things
but last seen clearly in 1226
by mediaeval people out in the sticks
astronomers argue that this solar gem
was the biblical star of Bethlehem
but this universe of which we're all part
enriches my mind and warms my heart

Sol-Sistere

The houl which turns the seasons
has brought winter round once more
the sun stands still twelve whole days
as yule logs burn so bright and warm
their flames banishing evil spirits
sweet ale and tales are shared with friends
homes are dressed in green and candles lit

This shortest day, so cold and raw
with its early sunset splendour
Sol-Sistere blessings to these lands
a time of wonderment and of awe
Capricorn fixed in skies above
astronomical winter's here
we welcome its return again
the old year has taken its leave
Saturnalia is reborn

With lighter days and warmth ahead
ritual gifts for ancient gods
bonfires light lands, vast and frozen
ginger snaps and saffron buns
waiting for the new day to dawn
glowing like a bright golden flame
bringing newfound hope and goodwill

(See overleaf for notes about Sol-Sistere)

Sol-Sistere Notes:

Houl, Norse mythology,
the wheel that turns the seasons, giving the name yule.
12 days of sun.
Celts and Romans believed that in mid-winter the sun stayed still
for 12 days
hence the 12 days of Christmas.
Yule logs.
Celtic and Norse tradition,
burning them warded off evil spirits.
Sol-sistere, Latin meaning sun stands still.
Saturnalia is the roman solstice festival.
Ginger snaps and saffron buns
Scandinavian Nordic traditional treats.

Snow Moon

Snow moon
bright in the night
winter's last

The boney moon
or hungry moon
in Cherokee

Moon traverses earth

Full when earth lies
'twixt sun and moon

Near 28 full days
final phase of 8

Moon shines brighter
and then fades
pale and sanguine

Moon Boy

Sprayed and tagged the moon is his muse
no blemishes left, a softer diffuse
as high as he can, moon low in the sphere
among the pale night clouds shining so clear
as the new moon comes he'll be ready to start
Banksy would smile at this young boy's art
twelve months now he's been fixing the moon
if you want to see him he'll be back again soon

Suddenly Spring

While I was out walking on a cold and sunny day
a flower had appeared in the grass along the way
I'm sure it wasn't there when I walked the day before
and as I stood wondering, I noticed many more
crocuses and daffodils, snowdrops, lilacs too
Decorate the floors of woodland walks in many hues

The sun it shines much longer now bringing welcome heat
nesting birds and working bees are such a daily treat
spawning frogs, newts and toads in shallow crystal ponds
just like magic come alive from woodland faerie wands
many fluffy frolicking lambs leaping leisurely
as delicate butterflies seek shade upon a tree

A shy reclusive hare fends off yet another male
the local inn, where I'll rest, with a cold glass of ale
the scent of apple blossom sweet flowers in full bloom
the smell of fresh cut grass from new mowed lawns fill my room
and as the sunlight fades I'm sat playing with my cat
and admire the stealth flight of the pipistrelle bat

Song Of The Morning

It's four in the morning
and the robin begins
his morning aria
soon after, the blackbird
takes centre stage,
loud and musical is he
and he loves to steal the show

A dunnock warbles
between the phrases
while blue tit and song thrush
add colour to the scene as
Mr.Magpie rattles
his drumming back beat

Dawn begins to filter through
the gaps between my curtains
sleep won't come to me now
so I lie back and listen some more
to the joyful sounds of life
And feel as if the world sighs
And takes a deep breath
before preparing for a new day

Full circle

A new rainbow deflecting refracted light
a spectrum bright arcing and facing our sun
oh if I could wrap myself completely
in it's colourful robes
like water colours across this horizon's spectral sphere

And then travel the stratosphere and twice around the sun
and stepping through the night sky
and then twice around the moon

I'd race along the Kármán Line
where earth's sky kisses outer space
and step slowly atop big cumulus clouds

Then watch glistening raindrops falling
on the green fields down below
before safely returning to my earthly home

Ode to Nick Drake;
(Borrowed lines)

Above that Fruit Tree you left behind
the sky is growing dim
Shimmering in the glow of the Pink Moon

Time spoke to you and you listened
so I took my lessons from you
The river man had no reply
when you spoke of lilac time?

I'll never know about the way that river flowed
perhaps it wasn't meant for you or me

And I, like you, know the way to blue
yet, in time, you found your rhyme
though I will wait at your gate, hoping like the blind
'til day is done at the sinking of the sun

And when that bird had flown
you had no place to call your home
I felt your sorrow, and sensed it in your cello song

I wish that I could see you in the crowd
I'd lend a hand and lift you to my place in the cloud

You told us of the fruit tree,
like fame, it won't flourish
'til it's stalk is in the ground
the world learned too late what you were really worth

And when I hear the city clock
and the city streets freeze,
Will they fall to their knees
and pray for warmth and green paper?

Yet still I curse where I come from and swear in the night
and feel like a remnant
of my own past,
I'll always find things are moving too fast

Now I just sit on the ground in your way
but it's too hard for me to fly
because as a poor boy
nobody really cared how steep my stairs

I think about your stories and your rhymes
but Saturday's sun has long since gone
though I weep for days gone by

Well now you're here to brighten my northern sky
and I hear you sing...
about loving you for your money
and loving you for your head
or loving you through the winter
and loving you 'til your dead
how I sobbed alone in my room

Again you solemnly sang
that Pink moon is on its way
and that none will stand so tall
because pink moon would get you all

Yeah, it's a pink moon...
and I smile every time I hear
you sing these sorrowful words
with your songs I'm in another place

Though when you're darker than the deepest sea
and you are searching for that place to be
I too feel weak in this need for you
but I can take the road that will see me though

But you, you were made to love magic
alas, you were lost in that magic many years ago
and now Mayfair's starry lights and golden throne
are down below and I'm on my own

Now I'm dressed in strange clothes of sand
and who can say that I that I stayed too long
I was left by the roadside alone with your songs
but this was my time of no reply

**Not Quite Right;
All The Madmen Revisited
(Tribute To David Bowie)**

In strange places dark and old
broken windows let in the cold
high walls that hide our shame
forgetting those who also came
electric convulsions numb my brain
strapped onto a bed again
ashen faces and hollow eyes
nothing seen in landscapes of lies
a corruption of souls never free
who's being protected, you or me?
just let me sink into this void
away from this hell of the paranoid

Musings On David Sylvian's Orpheus

From darkness to light
and renewal
metaphorical winds blow
within and without me is darkness
but I hope to see light

Do I stay the course or leave,
exit this journey?
I struggle with fear
of what you will hear

But it inspires my muse,
Orpheus in death-like slumber
as if in a final sleep
in his katabasis

On his back
in incubation
before disappearing
down to Hades' realm

There is great beauty
in all things, dark and light
nothing more to fear
it all fits into place

The past is washed away
in rituals of understanding
Orpheus, the initiate
will be here by my side

Bards were mystics,
mystics were priests
priests were healers
healers were initiates
Initiates were bards

But the joke played upon us
is ego and that's who we are,
in this sleepless world
where neither science,
religion or politics is real

The Last Farewell

Oh prima ballerina
you took your final bow
under the golden spotlight
spread your wings to fly
you hung up you ballet shoes
for the very last time
your dancing days are over
tears broke in your eyes
but you left the stage with pride
and flowers in your wake

Welcome To Dystopia

Evolution is in reverse
revolution, but not in your purse
constitution, nothing but a curse
destitution only makes it worse
only one life, you can't rehearse
it's not a song, with line and verse
life is a gamble they won't reimburse
angry mobs police can't disperse
old boys mocked, their response is terse
marriages over for better or worse
I can't stand the system, my feelings averse
no remedy now, my anger I nurse
the Satanist holds his crucifix inverse
the road is long that I must traverse
and mankind is killing this universe

Deepest Dreaming

Sunlight glaring blinding my eyes
A scene so surreal it could not be
or a lucid dream so vivid and wild
suspended in animation above
like floating inverted pyramids
what strange new metaphor is this?

Tip tentatively almost touches tip
casting amazing shadows
upon the water in which they float
foreboding sky, warns of coming storm
or perhaps a new world order dawning
if this is a dream then don't let me wake

I Love The Sky

I love the sky in autumn, ominously grey
dark as slate and menacingly heavy
like a scene from one of Turner's works
and the promise of a coming storm

I love the sky of an early spring morning
where the clouds are so high and pure
and the sun shines through as in a filter
as birds flit all around with purpose

I love the sky on a warm summer's eve
when the sun no longer threatens to burn
the flowers bask in the last of its rays
while I sip lemonade an begin to unwind

I love the sky in the depths of winter
when it looks as pale as it's ever been
its atmosphere is the stuff of dreams
it's the winter sky I love best of all

This Space

In this sacred realm I feel safe
this blessed space bathed in light
I'm a being of no spiritual faith
but somehow I feel I belong
this house of god or gods unknown
has calmed my mind and my body
my heart rate slows to a resting beat
as if in meditation I slip into a dream
I'm transported to another world
perhaps to another state of mind
fear and anxiety are strangers now
incense fills the air about me
warm breeze provides an atmosphere
an ambient scene of serenity, a bliss
I could gladly stay here for eternity
but I feel this place has finished with me
leaving, I thank whatever led me here
I'm a being of a certain spiritual faith
and a worshipper of this special place

Don't Rain On My Parade

Don't rain on my parade
before it has begun
why is it always you
who's out to spoil my fun?
all I ever wanted
was to strike out on my own
but all you've done is criticise,
it's all I've ever known
well, I'll have my parade,
my listening days are done
I'd love for you to come along,
if you'd only change your tone

The Enemy Within

Rage is my biggest enemy
ire, is always racing through me
then all I see is a red rag
there's never been a white flag
I just can't take this overload
my entire life's about to implode
hate, well that's very strong word
still, we all use it undeterred
how the hell can I return
all I've known is going to burn
nowhere to hide and no place go
I think my head's about to blow
life was hard, but at least I tried
guess I'll see you on the other side

Lowborn

Thy lowborn demon
of infernal realms
a calculating mind
and malicious warrior
deadly and stern,
pitiless and cruel
knower of black suns,
yon Soul devourer
most torturous fury,
I know thy philosophy
reader of all beings,
Anubis is thy guardian
spewing out remains
of the demonised
foul stench of death
emits from thy breath
yet I will smite thee
with mine own hands
and split thee clean in half
thy many eyes shall
turn red and weep
with thine own blood
victorious I shall rise
cut out thy black heart
feed thee to Anubis
and make him mine own
then raze all Hades
'til no more remains

The End Of The Dream

Two ghostly silent acrobatic cosmonauts
walking tightrope out in deepest space
they're fixing ubiquitous connectivity
a time signature that emotions convey
along bloodlines through dynasties wide
secrets of the universe readily revealed

When Daedalus wept with grief and guilt
as Icarus spiraled down from the sky
rhythms of earth shuddered and sighed
as if in mourning of what has passed
like exit wounds tearing the atmosphere
another rocket blasts into bright skies above

I Scorpion

A creature with the burning sting
Zeus' punishment for Orion's boast
Egyptian spirit, guardian for souls
on their journey to the other world
shamanic spirit scorpion guide
to psychedelic spiritual realms
where dreams are prophetic realities
my spirit animal's protective powers
ridding my old life of psychic clutter
transforming my body and my mind
some things must die to enable new life

Scorpion energy regenerates my soul
it guides and teaches me to see
so I can find the balance between
a spiritual solitude and mental desires
with totem creatures I never fear
life and death I readily embrace
resilient and adaptable, I go where I will
join me in this sacred passion dance of life

Wounded

Like a stealth bomber
undetected
under the radar
a Ninja warrior
thief in the night
I was defenseless
I didn't see you coming
no warning signs
mortally wounded
I reeled
as you poisoned
my heart and soul
mission accomplished

The Black Widow

The black widow takes the greatest of care
mixing her potions, she's an expert and how
no-one has ever known what she does there
three wealthy husbands she's buried now

to friends and neighbours, she's the sweetest soul
with a warm smile and a kind word for you
but she always has an ultimate goal
her eyes on new men and their money too

If you don't want to be victim number four
then you'd be wise to take note of my plea
when Ms.Widow comes knocking at your door
don't accept her invitation to tea

Child's Play

Is anything more sweet or free
than children
playing in the rain

Such energy
A joy to see
nothing lost
everything gained

Unaware in exciting times
soaking wet without a care

Skipping in puddles
chanting rhymes
no worries about slips or falls

If grown ups re-lived
those perfect days
we'd learn from them
the better way

Looking back
we'd change our ways
play in the rain

re-live and learn

Hummingbird

A vibrant flash of azure blue
and bright shimmering shades of green
no finer sight in any hue
and oh so small and delicate
that humming sound, a telling clue
swift beating wings hovering still
he dines on nectar fresh as dew
perfectly formed flying machine
the fairest bird that ever flew

Elephant On A Tightrope

We're talking past each other
not on the same train

Moving but nothing changes

Going through the motions
like robots in factories

We made promises
but couldn't keep them

I've always hated promises

I made a mess of you and me
like an elephant on a tightrope

I'm just about to fall

Goodbye my love

I won't send my address
I know you want to move on

So here's to brighter days

Wand'rin'
(Memories of Lee Marvin)

Under a wand'rin' star
I came into this life.
home's just a place too far
mem'ries of pain and strife

I'm never looking back
no matter where I roam
a road or a dirt track
is where I make my home

Cold snow in the winter
a camp fire's warm and bright
cruel sun in the summer
shady trees keep me right

Wand'rin' star, I see you
ev'ry new place I go
and when clouds spoil my view
you're there for me, I know

Limbo

I'm at a junction in my life
whatever that means
but the signals are down
probably been vandalised

Now which way do I turn?
I'm a born procrastinator
I don't do important decisions
convinced I'll make a bad one

Blindly, I step out onto the road
and it's a busy four way street

Many people like to look back
well, good for them, I suppose
rose tinted specs are not me
if I look back, I know I won't see
what the hell's in front of me

and like a lemming
over the cliff I'd go

So where do I go from here
the road not taken is overgrown
and besides, it's probably a minefield

So like a rabbit in a headlight
I'm stood here frozen
unable to think or move
waiting for the next bus
to come along and splat me
knowing my bad luck
the last one's already gone

I'm still here at this crossroads
waiting for who knows what
and I can't go forwards
but I won't go back

Broken

Bluer than Kind Of Blue
deeper than the abyss
colder than Oymyakon
locked inside of myself

Unreachable
Unchangeable
Breakable

Darker than The Great Nothing
desolate and empty
lost in a barren wilderness
far, far from myself

Deflated
Defeated
Damned

Moonlight Flit

I'm doing a flit by the light of the moon
along country roads, I should be there by noon
I'm in so much debt and can't pay my rent,
I've got nothing left, my savings are spent
a brand new start in a strange new town,
I'll look for work and try to settle down
I'll live within my means, take more care,
home cooked food and cut my own hair
it's taken some time but lessons I've learned,
I'm not spending money that I haven't earned

The Long Walk

Maundering
merrily
by myself
daydreaming

Listening
birds singing
endlessly
through the day

At midday
time to rest
under trees
in the shade

Near sunset
a dog fox
foraging
hears an owl

Darkness comes
moon is high
lights my way
to my door

Home again
tired and worn
days like this
worth it all

Gone

Our conversations
are released
into the air
swept away
on the breeze

I wish that I
could capture them
somehow
bring them back
to me

They're now fading
in my memory
some are lost
gone
forever

And now that you
are gone
I wish that I
could recall
our conversations

New Life

While walking in the woods today
soaking up the sounds of nature
a blinding flash of light appeared
right in front of me on the path ahead
as I grew closer I saw a vision of space
a deafening sound and a freezing blast
mesmerising and terrifying I didn't move

Was this a worm hole, in Einstein's work?
beyond the realms of normality and humanity?
tentatively, I stepped through this hole
why do this, I will never know
where will it take me, among the gods?
a Narnia or a lost Mayan world
could I return I wondered aloud?

Would I want to was my next thought
what I saw just blew my mind
familiar yet alien bright and warm
topography of the likes I'd never seen
I stand completely still for a moment
using all my senses I absorb all I can
will I be alone or will I find life like me?

And I wonder why I came to this place
I start to think if I was somehow chosen
or was my mind playing tricks anyway
a decision is made, I will not return
but I can't allow another human come here
we're killing our world, we'd do the same here
How can I hide or destroy this passage?

I don't believe in miracles and magic
I don't believe in gods or demons
but as I stood there with these thoughts
the light disappeared with an enormous flash
the hole was no more, the bridge had gone
stunned, I looked all about me again

Silence was replaced with the singing of birds
a breeze in the trees and sweet smell of flowers
I still don't know if I'm here all alone
but for as long as my life carries me on
I'd rather be here than where I came from
slowly I begin to explore this enchanting place
and bending to scoop water from a stream
I discover I'm being watched form afar

A human like being looking just like me
startled, I drop to the forest floor
but he beckons me over palms outstretched
trembling with nerves I step closer by inches
but as strange as it seems, I'm not afraid
as he draws closer I gasp, becoming aware
that the man I see looks exactly like me

He speaks softly, he knew I would come
and offers me food as we sit on the grass
then tells me of this new world I find myself in
that there are no gods, this creation's my own
a way to escape my lonely existence
this paradise is everything I want it to be
a realm in which pain and sorrow aren't known

Once I Was A Wildflower Meadow
(The Sad March Of Progress)

Once I was a wildflower meadow
providing life, shelter and healing herbs
all around me hedge and ancient woodland grew
together we all lived harmoniously

White clover grew among my grasses
buttercups, cocks foot, dock and vetch
common orchids and twayblades proud
the iconic bluebells carpeted the woods in spring

All year round, life's art and music at work
birds, beasts and insects made their homes
strange creatures lay down in my long grasses
with pledges of their undying love

One day deep, loud rumbles broke my peace
many animals and birds froze then fled
those that could not, were trampled dead
and a strange eerie atmosphere hung in the air

My beautiful features were then torn apart
my warm earth, now bare, cut deep and wide
death came to those I had loved and nurtured
nothing but darkness and strange creatures all around

More strange creatures now and more deep cuts
and then my body felt heavy, crushed and broken
I could no longer breath in nature's ways
and alien shapes began to appear on my skin

Now I only breath in patches of green squares
and small areas where flowers now grow
not my kin folk from when I was meadow
but species unknown and, not good for my earth

Soon I'm overrun by these strange creatures
they are loud, polluting and cut my grasses short
my soul has died along with my long lost kin
but who will mourn my passing or remember me?

Ivo and Laria.

In the furthest reaches of the enchanted forest
where light never penetrates the still darkness,
Ivo and Laria went hunting and frolicking
against the strict orders of their elders and sages
there they shot at any creatures they could find
killing for fun, shooting arrows hither and thither
trampling delicate insects, plants and the smallest of sprites
and then killed a boar with a silver dagger
smeared his blood over one another's bodies
and dedicated his sacrifice in their own names
proclaiming themselves as god and goddess of all
before consummating their carnal lust
'neath the sacred elm, ash and oak

Outraged, the creatures, trees and spirits of the forest
pleaded with the goddess of nature Karaenin to act
she, on hearing their plight flew swift as an owl
to the place where they lay together in their ecstasy
revealed herself and demanded they bow before her
begging forgiveness for their crimes
in an act of defiance and hubris, Ivo said unto her
"it is you who should bow to us, we are gods of all"
laughing, Laria mocked her actions and her words

But in a calm voice Karaenin softly uttered these words
"you have defiled this sacred place your ancestors held dear
your deeds have offended the creatures of this holy place of nature
the plants and the trees cried out at the sight of your shame
and still you show no guilt and no remorse."
turning three times and then raising her hands to the skies
she pronounced that she will turn them both into dead trees,
he would become oak and she would be elm
and no life shall grow upon them nor seek shelter upon them
Laria ran to Ivo for protection but it was of no use

And just as they embraced the curse began to take hold
their flesh began to crack and turn to bark
and their feet became rooted deep into the earth

they cried out in pain as they finally succumbed
forever bound to nature but no longer of her
it is here they can be found ten thousand years on
in the enchanted forest now known as lover's tree woods
all around this strange eerie but beautiful scene in the woods
the creatures, spirits and nature live in close harmony
retelling the tales from eons ago to any human soul
who happens by with a curious eye and an open mind

Blodeuwedd - Owl Goddess

She comes nightly in dreams to me
reminds me to see through darkness
to listen to my inner voice
Blodeuwedd, oh flower faced one
Welsh Owl Goddess so wise and true
of Math and Gwydion are you
as told in the Mabinogi
icon for women for all time
bound by oaths not of their choosing
all transpersonal energies
and all those things universal
through you alone are redefined
into the forces of all life
you, our holy nine-fold goddess
of western isles of paradise
goddess of the ceremonies
bless all those who suffer in fear
with wisdom, love and consciousness
and with patient observation
with your eyes you see all there is
your ears hear all things unuttered
your mystic heart heals all good things
unknown to all but the holy
she comes nightly in dreams to me
and tells me not to fear my dreams

Biography:

George Mansell was born in Washington
in the North East of England in 1965,
where he spent his formative years.
Being half Scottish, he has many fond memories
of annual holidays in St. Andrews, Fife.
George completed his degree in history
in South Wales in 2003, after transferring from the
University Of Sunderland.
Wales, with its beautiful valleys and mountains,
this nation's history and Celtic heritage
would go on to become major influences
on his poems and prose included in this book.
His other passions, including music
and the natural world,
also feature prominently in his writing.
His first poem "Not Here" was written
during a moment of dark sadness
and a feeling of isolation.
He didn't write again for almost a year,
and only then after a close friend
(now herself a published poet)
showed him her work.
He began to write poems and prose
as a means of dealing
with his past and his feelings
and finds it immersive and therapeutic.
Many of his poems are short
and don't follow any particular form,
which George thinks may be a result
of him having ADHD.
"From The Other Side Of My Mind"
is George's first book.

George Mansell

Printed in Great Britain
by Amazon